Big Logs!

Illustrated by The Artful Doodlers

Random House New York
Thomas the Tank Engine & Friends™

CREATED BY BRITT ALLCROFT

Based on The Railway Series by The Reverend W Awdry. © 2010 Gullane (Thomas) LLC.
Thomas the Tank Engine & Friends and Thomas & Friends are trademarks of Gullane (Thomas) Limited.
HIT and the HIT Entertainment logo are trademarks of HIT Entertainment Limited.
All rights reserved. Published in the United States by Random House Children's Books, a division of Random House, Inc., 1745 Broadway,
New York, NY 10019, and in Canada by Random House of Canada Limited, Toronto. Step into Reading, Random House, and the
Random House colophon are registered trademarks of Random House, Inc.
www.stepintoreading.com   www.randomhouse.com/kids   www.thomasandfriends.com

Educators and librarians, for a variety of teaching tools, visit us at
www.randomhouse.com/teachers
ISBN: 978-0-375-85368-5   MANUFACTURED IN CHINA

HiT entertainment

Gordon.

Gordon is big!

Logs.

Big logs!

Gordon got big logs.

Gordon has to go.

He has a lot of logs!

It is hot!

Gordon is hot.

Go, Gordon, go!

A jam!

Gordon can not go.

Gordon is hot.

Dan.

Dan got the big logs.

Dan is hot.

No jam.

Time to go.

Go, Gordon, go!

Gordon is not hot.

Gordon is happy.

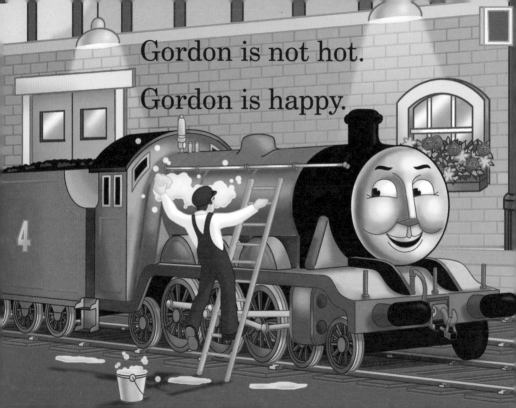